Welcome To Dark Dale

LIANA BROOKS

OTHER WORKS

HEROES AND VILLAINS

Even Villains Fall In Love
Even Villains Go To The Movies
Even Villains Have Interns
Even Villains Play The Hero (books 1 – 3 omnibus)
The Polar Terror

FLEET OF MALIK

Bodies In Motion
Change of Momentum
For Every Action (forthcoming)

SHORTER WORKS

All I Want For Christmas Is A Werewolf
Darkness and Good
Fey Lights
Prime Sensations

Find other works by the author at
www.lianabrooks.com

Welcome To Dark Dale

INKLET #31

LIANA BROOKS

Inkprint PRESS

www.inkprintpress.com

Print ISBN: 978-1-925825-36-7
eBook ISBN: 9781393290698

www.inkprintpress.com

National Library of Australia Cataloguing-in-Publication Data
Brooks, Liana 1982 –
Welcome To Dark Dale
38 p.
ISBN: 978-1-925825-36-7
Inkprint Press, Canberra, Australia
1. Fiction—Fantasy—Action & Adventure 2. Fiction—Short Stories

First Print Edition: April 2020
Cover image © Sandra Kaas via Unsplash
Cover design © Inkprint Press
Interior art © Amy Laurens

WELCOME
TO DARK
DALE xx

WELCOME TO DARK DALE

THE SIGN WAS BROKEN. FRAGMENTS LAY on the ground, splintered and splattered with blood. What remained of the rotting stump in the ground was charred and gnawed on; teethed on, I corrected myself. There was still a tooth sticking out of the wood.

Marzrels went through several sets of teeth as babies—larvae? They were carnivorous worms and I'd never stopped to ask one what it called its young.

Dinner maybe. But probably breakfast. Just another joy of Dark Dale.

A shadow caught my eye: a small, yellow scorpion no bigger than my thumb, darting away. I stepped on it.

Those I occasionally called friends laughed at my odd footwear. They told me on numerous drunken occasions that I'd do better to leave the iron out of my boots and run faster. As I lifted my foot and used a second dagger to dig out the still-wriggling arachnid, I yet again disagreed with them.

I killed the wriggler and left the body in the dust. One didn't survive the Dale by being kind and loving.

Of course, I'd never asked anyone else about surviving the Dale; as far as I knew, I was the only one who could make the claim. Horrific death was about as native to the Dale as marzrels.

I sauntered toward my destination, a nondescript rock of little intrinsic value, slashing at bushes and stabbing at shadows. The bushes burned and the sand crackled under the loving brush of my sword of fire.

Most people liked to collect mementos of their adventures. The average sword-for-hire collected gold; others took bones, teeth, ears, treasure, whatever caught their fancy. A fair number in this region collected skulls.

I collected swords. The swords of slain heroes, and I'd killed every one. And because I knew the weapon I carried had already failed one protagonist, I also carried daggers.

At the rock, I paused and growled. This was the part of visiting the Dale that I didn't like.

"I am she that is summoned. I am she that answers." I recited the chant from memory, paying minimal attention as the rock steamed and smoked. The smoke coalesced and formed into an ashen-skinned demon with glowing silver eyes.

"Took you long enough didn't it?" the creature demanded petulantly. "Do you know how long I've been waiting?"

"Two days," I guessed, since I had only received the summons two days ago—in the middle of a barroom brawl no less, which had been most inconvenient. "You were here last time. Make someone in the council mad, did we?"

The demon sniffed. "You know not of what you speak, mortal!"

"Of course I know of what I speak, and don't call me mortal unless you intend to prove the point." My free hand wandered closer to the abyssal whip I had picked off the body of a half-eaten necromancer.

Some people would never learn to leave well enough alone. At least not in this life.

"You will die!" the demon cried.

Demons did this sort of thing; it was habit more than anything else and not something that had particularly bothered me once I realized they all did it. I was nearly eight when that happened. Some little girls played with dolls, or horses, or looms, or swords, but I was deprived, forced to play with demons because I lacked parental supervision and income.

"You'll die too, eventually," I observed. "Does that make you mortal?"

"Of course not." The demon peered at me. "One of these days I'm going to make you flinch."

"Don't count on it," I advised.

It shrugged. "Here." It held out a miniature portrait and dropped it at my feet. "Kill this."

I picked up the likeness of a brawny man. "Nicely painted. Oils?"

"Oils?" the demon asked. "How should I know?"

"You didn't paint this?" I looked at him suspiciously. Having a demon hire me was not unheard of, but if this demon was hiring me for its own reasons, no other creature should have painted the likeness.

"It was given to me by the council." The demon looked as apologetic as it could.

"This is a council assignment?" The answer was important: it affected pay.

I always charged the council more. It was spite, and I'd be the first to admit it.

I didn't like the council. One of the idiots on it sired me—possibly mothered me, I wasn't quite sure. But I was spawned by one of them and they'd dropped me in the mortal realm with no more than a spell book and a handful of silver. Hardly decent parenting, in my book. Gold was what loving parents gave to their spawn—or offspring, species-dependent.

The demon rubbed the bald space between its horns. "You won't charge too much, will you?"

"For a rush job on a brawny barbarian?" I tossed the miniature in the
air and caught it thoughtfully. The demon's silver eyes followed the portrait.
"Triple my usual rates for a rush job.
Plus the weight of the hero in gold."

His eyes snapped to my face. "Out-
rageous! You worked for the liche in
the summer valley for a quarter of that
for the same sort of outlander!"

I tossed the portrait to the demon
and shrugged. "Then find another as-
sassin. If you can find one who will
survive."

That was my trump card every time.
No one survived Dark Dale. Those that
didn't die outright were turned. Some
were zombies, some liches, others hid-
eous constructs of the Madness, souls
ripped and torn beyond recognition.
The lucky ones (or unlucky, depending
on your moral outlook) were turned
into lesser demons: imps, succubae,
incubi, and other half-mad things that

did the bidding of the powerful. They would never be true demons, not with parts of their human souls intact, but they lived like demons.

"Double plus the weight," the demon bargained.

"Triple plus the weight." I stood firm. "You won't be able to find anyone else."

The demon grumbled something foul under its breath.

"Just tell yourself it comes out of the council's treasury, not yours."

The demon tossed its head in a nod. "Not my soul," it muttered. "Find the hero. Kill the hero. And your pay will arrive as usual."

"Good enough," I agreed placidly. Most humans don't know that demons are actually bound by their words—unlike humans, who can lie constantly without punishment. No blood or vows are needed, just a firmly-worded agreement.

The demon's promise was contingent on my finding and killing the hero, but since I *would* find and kill said hero, there was no problem. "How many days ahead is this hero?"

The demon held up three pointed talons. "He nears the east gate even now. Within two moonrises he will have reached the portal."

"Are you not attacking him?" I asked with more suspicion than usual.

"We have thrown everything at him since he arrived."

"The east gate is nearly impossible to reach unless you have a demon guide," I noted. "Does he have a demon guide?"

"No." The ashen demon squirmed.

"Tell me," I ordered.

"He is impervious to magic. He nulls it. Nothing we do works." The demon, with its monstrous horns, bulging muscles and venomed talons, pouted.

I sheathed my sword of fire and pulled out a sharp iron spike. "Is he mortal or a demigod?"

"Mortal, most assuredly."

I gave the demon a pointed look.

"Probably mortal," it amended with an apologetic shrug. "No divine influence has been seen on him."

"Well, that at least is encouraging." I traded my iron dagger for my favorite offhand weapon: a sword breaker.

There are two kinds of sword breakers readily available for those who want to crush their enemies and deprive them of hope. The first is the traditional iron rod with no sharp edge. It's heavy, sword-length, and if you strike hard enough, swords break.

The second is a long dagger with a sharp edge on one side and a deep-set jagged edge on the other side. You catch your opponent's weapon in the deep-set serrations and twist.

Snap!

Such a lovely sound and so useful when you are forced into confrontation with berserkers, especially those who tie their souls to their blades. The look of panic as they realize their pride has killed them is priceless.

Well, no, not priceless; I can put a price on anything.

"Well," I told the demon. "I'd better get going then." I gave it a sardonic smile. "Tell the Council hi from me."

It glared at me. "Tell them yourself." Smoke puffed and the demon vanished.

I rolled my eyes at the theatrics and hefted my sword. Time to give our barbarian friend a nice old Dark Dale welcome—the traditional way.

THE MAKING OF *WELCOME TO DARK DALE*

"Welcome To Dark Dale"—I could see the sign in my head, smell the dry wood and the hot desert. Feel the sun burning my face and the sand scratching at my legs. But I wasn't sure where it would go from there.

The world of Dark Dale unfolded oddly, in fits and spurts. At one time I played with the idea of writing a series there, but other plots distracted me. In the end all that was left was a moment in the desert.

FEY LIGHTS

DARK WATER WRITHED OVER THE SHIP'S deck, a living thing hunting for prey, stinging like acid where it touched bare skin. Jeani stumbled over the guts of her ship, swearing in every language she knew. Her foot fell through a hole in the deck created by the crash. Hot metal gouged her leg as tears ran down her cheeks.

I don't want to die like this. There has to be a way out.

There is *a way out. The same way the water is coming in.*

Running was out of the question. Half-limping, half-swimming through the rising water, Jeani forced herself back to the rear of the ship, navigating by touch and the weak glow of the emergency lights that hadn't burst, back to the gaping wound that was once the engine room and secondary hold. Pressure from the rapid descent into the gravity well and the gushing water warped the frame, creating a strong current. Jeani grabbed the free-fall handle near the emergency door and pressed her free hand to the glowing lock.

Nothing.

She tried yanking the override.

Nothing.

She kicked the door with her good leg.

Pressure sent the door flying inwards at the head of a tidal wave. Jeani gasped for air and went under. Seconds ticked away as she grappled blindly for the next free-fall handle, the current tugging at her.

The hand-hold slipped out of her grip. She pushed up once, bumping her head against the high ceiling of the engine room as she gasped for air. The current swirled under her, pulling her down into the darkness.

Saltwater stung her face. She shuddered as something nipped at her bleeding leg. Ignoring the pain, she clawed at the water until she broke through and gasped in the alien atmosphere. Water crashed over her in the darkness.

Rough, warm sand rubbed against her skin. Sucking in a lungful of the oxygen-rich air, Jeani flipped onto her stomach and pulled herself away from the water. It lapped at her legs, a wayward lover begging her to return.

She laughed as she looked at the strange stars overhead. Her lungs burned, her leg ached, she was shaking with delayed shock, but she was alive. "See, Hothi, I told you I wasn't going to die that easy."

Dominique pushed through the crowd and looked down at the beach.

"Could be a Lander," Gregor said as he adjusted his cap. "Saw the prison ships sailing past this last moon. Could be a Lander," he repeated with a final snort.

A knife waved past Dominique's face, stabbing toward the figure on the beach. "'Twere wedding lights last night. Lit up the sky with fire, set the trees to burning," said Beau.

"'Tain't no fire touched the trees. Trees are fine," Gregor argued. "'Tis a Lander."

"Fey fire," someone said behind him. "Fey burn things with cold fire." A fist hit Dominique's shoulder. "Fey can turn a man's bones to ice. They summon monsters from the deep."

One of the women crossed her fingers and made the sign of the arch to ward off the ill will of the deep dwellers.

"Landers bring plague," Adrian said grimly. He too tapped Dominique's shoulder. "We can't let a Lander near the village."

"We's best shooting it from here," Gregor said.

Another shook his head. "Arrows can't touch fey."

"You volunteering to go down there to slit its throat?" Gregor demanded.

"Such a thing to ask a man! I've got kin, I have."

There was the sound of shuffling feet. A cool sea breeze wrapped around Dominique's legs as the crowd parted. He filled their silence with imagined conversations.

"He's a Lander," one would say in the Silent way of the island-born. *"Got no kin nor woman of his own, does he,"* someone else would murmur.

Dominique kept the snarl he felt forming in his throat from escaping.

"Will you go?" Adrian whispered,

confirming his suspicions. "None will make you, if you say no."

"You'll go?" Dominique asked with a half-smile. Adrian wasn't a bad man. Island born, birthed in the sea, born running on the beach and listening to the waves.

The island-born claimed the waves spoke back to those that listened. The saltwater seeped into their blood so they could hear the thoughts of others like they heard the song of the ocean. Like all the island born, Adrian had no trouble believing every infamy laid against the Landers who lived on the far side of the ocean, in the land of the tyrant.

Adrian shrugged. "Better to slit the Lander's throat on the beach than let it breathe on a child in the village. We'll all die of black blood and fever before the tide is high."

"I'll go," Dominique said, loud enough for his voice to carry to the back of the crowd. "I'll go see to the Lander. I'll send him down to the docks in the south. He can find work there if he likes."

"What if it be fey?" Gregor asked, eyes wide.

Dominique studied the lone figure on the distant sand below, a sad creature sprawled under the hot morning sun. "The fey have a treaty with the Tyrant of Urull. The first tyrant traded his soul for the secrets of the fey lights—wedding lights," he corrected himself, using the island-born term. "The first tyrant lost his mind when the fey showed him the wonders of their world. Men that could turn into dogs. Deep monsters that could walk as men. Women so beautiful that they could suck the soul of a man as he walked past, steal his life with a kiss.

"The tyrants all have made a pact with the fey, traded their subjects to the fey for their favor, but they've never let the fey roam the lands. No fey walk outside the tyrant's gates in Urull. No fey step on the white sands of the islands."

"Maybe this one is outcast," Beau said. "A prisoner, like all the other Landers sent here."

"You've got a leak in your hull," Adrian said, punching Beau in the arm. "You think the tyrant could make a prisoner out of the fey? You think a man could keep one of them under lock and key?"

"But... wedding lights!" Beau lookeded to Dominique for support. "The lights haven't touched our sky in years."

"No one's been out walking in years," Dominique said. "Who was out last night?" He turned and scanned the crowd.

Hardy folk, the island-born. They wore homespun cloth, britches of old sail cloth traded from down the coast, filigree gold necklaces twined around shells and sea gems. All of them came from Lander families at some point in their history, Landers who had either escaped the tyrants, or been banished to a slow death on the distant islands, depending on who you asked.

But the islands were in their blood now. They spoke in Silence, and left him an outcast. The women looked away from him, the older men met his gaze, and one boy blushed. "Tris? Were you out walking last night?"

The boy with dark eyes and a thatch of red hair looked up. "May have been. What's it to you?"

Someone chuckled.

"Explains the wedding lights," Gregor muttered. "You still ought to slit the throat first. That one's not going to give you any answer you'll be wanting."

Keep reading! Head to
www.lianabrooks.com/books/short-stories/
to buy your copy now!

ABOUT THE AUTHOR

LIANA BROOKS was born in California and raised in the American South-West where she developed an appreciation for deserts, cactus, and chilies. She still enjoys driving through the desert sometimes and looking up at the infinity of stars overhead. It's a beautiful place.

When she isn't traveling, Liana enjoys writing science fiction in every form, from sprawling space operas (*Fleet of Malik*) to the antics of super-hero families (*Heroes and Villains*).

You can learn more about her and her books at www.LianaBrooks.com.

INKLETS

Collect them all! Released on the 1st and 15th of each month.

INKLET #031
Welcome to Dark Dale
LIANA BROOKS

INKLET #032
When War Came to Town
A Powers Story
AMY LAURENS

INKLET #033
Not Fantasy
AMY LAURENS

INKLET #034
Courting the Winter Prince
LIANA BROOKS

INKLET #035
At the Home of the Winter King
A Storm Foxes Story
AMY LAURENS

INKLET #036
With This Ring
AMY LAURENS

INKLET #037
Venus &
Seven Reasons I Said No
LIANA BROOKS

INKLET #038
OATH KEEPER
AMY LAURENS

INKLET #039
FORGET
A Powers Story
AMY LAURENS

INKLET #040
NOT QUITE
Cinderella
LIANA BROOKS

INKLET #041
ONE BAD MAN
AMY LAURENS

DOUBLE ISSUE
INKLET #042
The Claustrophobia
Of Loneliness &
Adam, Be A Star
AMY LAURENS

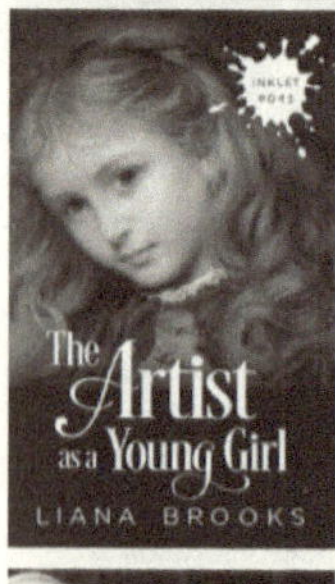

INKLET #043
The Artist
as a Young Girl
LIANA BROOKS

INKLET #044
CONFESSIONS
AMY LAURENS

INKLET #045
But For Snow
A Kaditeos Story
AMY LAURENS

INKLET #046
The Boy
Named NO
LIANA BROOKS

INKLET #047
Anamata
AMY LAURENS

INKLET #048
A Wolf FOR
Christmas
AMY LAURENS